For perplexed parents everywhere - C.C.

First published in 2000 by Macmillan Children's Books, London
First dual language publication 2002 by Mantra Lingua
All rights reserved

Mantra Lingua
5 Alexandra Grove, London N12 8NU
www.mantralingua.com

ہم اِس روتے بسورتے بچے کے ساتھ کیا کریں؟

What Shall We Do With The **BOO HOO BABY?**

by Cressida Cowell

Illustrated by Ingrid Godon

Urdu translation by Qamar Zamani

Mantra Lingua

بچہ بولا،

The baby said,

"چی ہیاؤں، چی ہیاؤں!"

"Boo-hoo-hoo!"

"قیس؟"
بطخ بولی۔

"Quack?"
said the duck.

ہم اِس روتے بسورتے بچے کے ساتھ کیا کریں؟

What shall we do with
the boo-hoo baby?

"اِس کو دودھ پلاؤ" کتے نے کہا۔

"Feed him," said the dog.

So they ted the baby.

لہذا، اُنہوں نے اُس کو خوراک دی۔

"میاؤں!"
بلی نے کہا۔

"Miaow!"
said the cat.

"بھُوں، بھُوں!"
کتّا بھونکا۔

"Bow-wow!"
said the dog.

"قَیس!"
بطخ بولی۔

"Quack!"
said the duck.

"مُووو!"
گائے بولی،

"Moo!"
said the cow,

اور۔۔۔

and...

بچہ بولا،

"چی ہیاؤں، چی ہیاؤں!"

"Boo-hoo-hoo!"
said the baby.

ہم اِس روتے بسورتے
بچے کے ساتھ کیا کریں؟
"اِس کو نہلاؤ،"
بلی نے کہا۔

What shall we do with
the boo-hoo baby?
"Bath him,"
said the cat.

لہذا، اُمّہوں نے بچّے کو نہلایا۔

So they bathed the baby.

"قیں!"
بطخ بولی۔

"Quack!"
said the duck.

"بھُوں، بھُوں!"
کتا بھونکا۔

"Bow-wow!"
said the dog.

"میاؤں!"
بلی نے کہا۔

"Miaow!"
said the cat.

لہذا، اُنہوں نے بچے کو کھیل سے بہلایا۔

So they played with the baby.

"قیس!"
بطخ بولی۔

"Quack!"
said the duck.

"بھُوں، بھُوں!"
کتا بھونکا۔

"Bow-wow!"
said the dog.

"میاؤں!"
بلی نے کہا۔

"Miaow!"
said the cat.

"مُووو!"
گائے بولی،

"Moo!"
said the cow,

اور...

and...

So they put him to bed.

"میاؤں!"

بلی نے کہا۔

"*Miaow!*"
said the cat.

لہٰذا، اُنہوں نے اُس کو بستر میں سُلا دیا۔

"موُووو!"
گائے بولی،

"قیں!"
بطخ بولی۔

"بھوُں، بھوُں!"
کتا بھونکا۔

"Moo!"
said the cow,

"Quack!"
said the duck.

"Bow-wow!"
said the dog.

اور...

and...

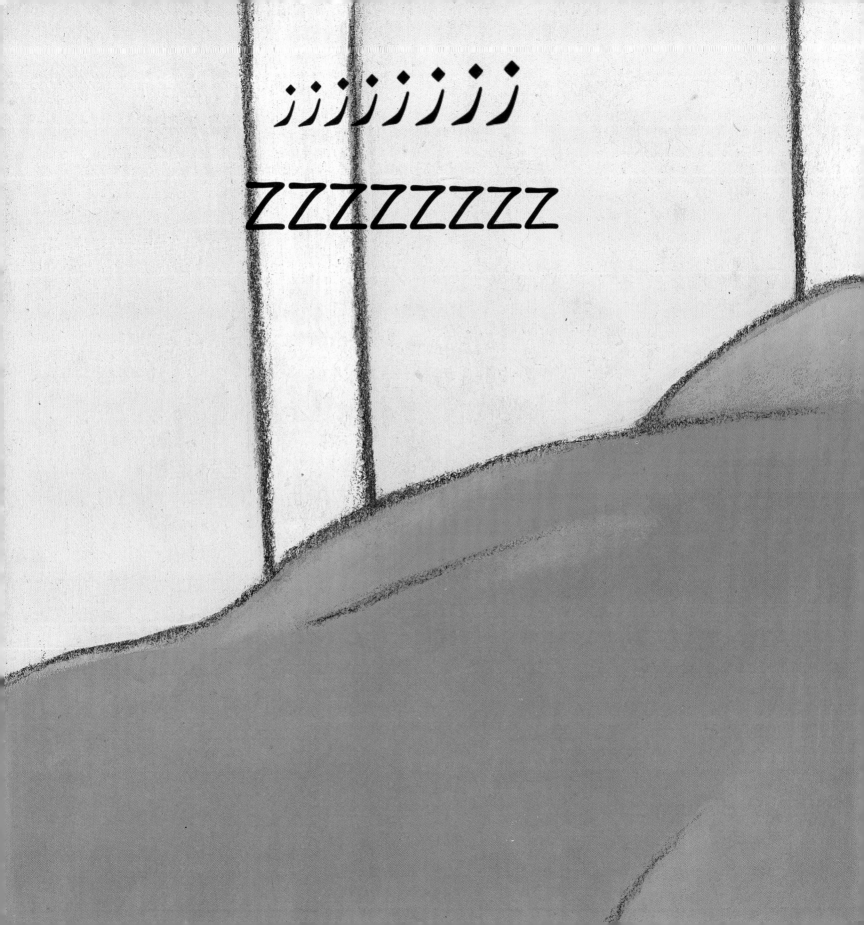

بچہ بولا۔

said the baby.